Romeo and Juliet

A Shakespeare Story

RETOLD BY ANDREW MATTHEWS
ILLUSTRATED BY TONY ROSS

ORCHARD BOOKS

To Leila, with love
A.M.

For Mike and Sue
T.R.

ORCHARD BOOKS
338 Euston Road, London NW1 3BH
Orchard Books Australia
Hachette Children's Books
Level 17/207, Kent St, Sydney, NSW 2000
This text was first published in Great Britain in the form of
a gift collection called *The Orchard Book of Shakespeare Stories*,
illustrated by Angela Barrett in 2001.
This edition first published in hardback in Great Britain in 2002
First paperback publication 2003
Text © Andrew Matthews 2001
Illustrations © Tony Ross 2002
The rights of Andrew Matthews to be identified as the author and
Tony Ross as the illustrator of this work have been asserted by them in
accordance with the Copyright, Designs, and Patents Act, 1988.
ISBN 978 1 84121 336 1 (paperback)
3 5 7 9 10 8 6 4 (paperback)
A CIP catalogue record for this book is available
from the British Library.
Printed in China

Contents

Cast List

Juliet

Daughter of Lord Capulet

Romeo

Son of Lord Montague

Mercutio

Friend to Romeo

Benvolio

Friend and cousin to Romeo

Tybalt

Cousin to Juliet

Nurse to Juliet

Friar Lawrence

Lord Capulet

The Prince of Verona

A Monk
Messenger to
Friar Lawrence

The Scene

Verona in the fifteenth century.

But soft, what light through yonder
window breaks?
It is the east, and Juliet is the sun.

Romeo; II.i.

Romeo and Juliet

On that warm summer's evening, the Capulet house was the brightest place in Verona. The walls of the ballroom were hung with silk tapestries, and candle-light from a dozen crystal chandeliers threw rainbows on to the heads of the masked dancers as they twirled through the music and laughter that filled the air.

On one side of the room, near a table laden with food and drink, stood a young girl, Juliet, the daughter of Lord and Lady Capulet. She had removed her mask and loosened her black hair so that it hung about her shoulders. Her face, flushed from the heat of the dance, was radiant

and her beauty was obvious to all who looked at her. She seemed unaware that someone was watching her.

A few steps away, a young man stood gazing at her. He had never seen such loveliness before in his whole life.

'Surely I must be mistaken!' he thought. 'Surely, if I look a second time, I will find that her eyes are too close together, her nose too long or her mouth too wide!' Moving slowly towards her, as one in a trance, the young man lifted his mask so that he could see Juliet more clearly – and the more he gazed at her, the more perfect her face seemed.

Almost without thinking, Romeo
pushed his way towards Juliet until he
found himself standing at her side. Gently
he took her hand.

Juliet turned her head, her soft brown
eyes wide with surprise.

✳ ✳ ✳

On the other side of the room, Tybalt, Lord Capulet's fiery young nephew, recognised the young man who was holding Juliet's hand, and strode angrily towards the door; but just as he was about to leave, his uncle caught him by the sleeve.

"Where are you going?" asked Lord Capulet.

"To fetch my rapier," Tybalt replied. "Lord Montague's son, Romeo, has dared to enter the house!"

"Leave him!" said Lord Capulet.

There was a terrible feud between the Capulets and the Montagues and the Prince of Verona had forbidden any more fighting between the two families, on pain of death.

Tybalt's face was ashen with rage. "But tomorrow, Romeo will boast to his friends about how he danced at the Capulets' ball and escaped without being noticed! He will make us look like fools!"

Lord Capulet put his hands on Tybalt's shoulders, forcing him to stop and listen.

"I hate the Montagues as deeply as you do, Tybalt," he said. "Our two families have been at war with each other for as long as anyone can remember – but the Prince's word is law in this city, and there is to be no more fighting – you understand? Now, if you cannot keep your temper like a man, go to your room and sulk like a boy!"

Tybalt broke free from his uncle's grasp
and glared across the room at Romeo.
"You will pay for this one day, Montague!"
he vowed softly. "I will make you pay!"

* * *

Juliet glanced at the young man beside her, at his glossy brown hair and startlingly grey eyes that were filled with shyness and wonder. His mouth was curved in a half-smile, and though it made her blush to look, Juliet found that she could not take her eyes from his face, or her hand from his.

"My lady," Romeo said, "if my hand has offended yours by holding it, please forgive me."

"My hand is not offended, sir," said Juliet, smiling at him, "and nor am I."

Some power that neither of them understood had drawn them together like a moth to a flame. They kissed and the ballroom, the musicians and dancers seemed to disappear, leaving them feeling as though they were the only two people in the world.

When their lips parted, Romeo looked at Juliet and thought, 'All those other times, when I thought I was in love, I was like a child playing a game. This time I am truly in love – I wonder, could she possibly feel the same?'

Before he could ask, an elderly woman bustled up to them. "My lady," she said to Juliet, "your mother is asking for you."

Juliet frowned, shrugged helplessly at Romeo, then turned and walked away.

Romeo caught the old woman by the arm. "Do you know that lady?" he demanded.

"Why, sir, she is Juliet, Lord Capulet's daughter," said the woman. "I've been her nurse since she was a baby. And I know who you are, too, young man. Take my advice and leave this house, before there's trouble!"

✳ ✳ ✳

That night Juliet couldn't get to sleep. She could only think of Romeo. It was warm and the moonlight was shining on the trees in the orchard below. Juliet stepped out onto her balcony, but she was so troubled by what her nurse had told her, that she hardly noticed how lovely the orchard looked.

"How can I be in love with someone I ought to hate?" she sighed. "Oh, Romeo, why did you have to be a Montague? If you had been born with any other name, I could tell you how much I love you!"

Romeo stepped out of the shadows of the trees into the moonlight. "Call me your love," he said. "It is the only name I want!"

Juliet looked down from her balcony and gasped. "How did you get here? If anyone catches you, they will kill you!"

"I climbed the orchard wall," said Romeo. "I had to see you again! I loved you the moment I first saw you, and I wanted to know if you felt the same."

Juliet's face brightened with joy, then darkened into doubt. "How can I be sure of your love?" she said. "How can I be sure that you will not forget me as soon as tonight is over?" Romeo looked up into Juliet's eyes and saw the way the moonlight shone in them. He knew he would never love anyone else.

23

"Meet me at Friar Lawrence's chapel at noon tomorrow, and we shall be married!" Romeo declared.

"Married?" laughed Juliet. "But we have only just met! And what will our parents say?"

"Do we need to meet more than once to know that our love is strong, and real?" said Romeo. "Must we live apart because of our families' hatred?"

A part of Juliet knew that for them to marry would be mad and impossible, but another part of her knew that if she sent Romeo away now, she might never see him again, and she wasn't sure she could bear that. "Yes!" she said. "Yes, I believe what we feel for each other is true! And yes, I'll meet you tomorrow at the chapel at noon!"

So, the next day Romeo and Juliet were married.

＊ ＊ ＊

The bell in the clock tower of the cathedral
tolled twice. The main square of Verona
sweltered in the hot sunshine and the air
shimmered. Two young men were lounging
beside a fountain and the taller
of the two, Romeo's
closest friend,
Mercutio,
dipped a
handkerchief
into the water
and mopped
his face.
"Where is he?"
he demanded
tetchily. "He
should have been
here an hour ago!"

His companion, Romeo's cousin, Benvolio, smiled at Mercutio's impatience. "Some important business must have detained him," he said.

"A pair of pretty eyes, more like!" snorted Mercutio. But as he glanced across the square, he saw Romeo hurrying towards them. "At last!" Mercutio said sarcastically, "I was beginning to think that the Queen of the Fairies had carried you off in your sleep!"

"I have great news!" said Romeo. "But you must promise to keep it a secret!"

Mercutio looked curiously at his friend. "Oh?" he said.

"I am in love," said Romeo.

Benvolio laughed; Mercutio groaned and shook his head. "You are always in love!" he cried. "A girl only has to look at you sideways to make you fall for her."

"It's more than that this time," said Romeo. "I am in love with…"

"Romeo!" interrupted a harsh voice.

Romeo turned, and saw Tybalt with a group of sneering Capulets. Tybalt's right hand was resting on the hilt of his sword. "You were at my family's house last night," he said. "Now you must pay for your insolence. Draw your sword!"

Romeo's eyes flashed with anger, then grew calm. "I will not fight you, Tybalt," he said. "It would be like fighting one of my own family."

"Why, you milksop!" jeered Tybalt. "You're as cowardly as the rest of the Montagues."

"Romeo!" gasped Mercutio. "Are you going to stand and do nothing while he insults your family?"

"I must," said Romeo. "You don't understand. I have no choice…"

"But I do!" snarled Mercutio.

His rapier flashed in the sunlight as he drew it. "If you want a fight, Tybalt, I'm your man!" he cried.

In a movement too fast to follow, Tybalt brought out his sword and the two young men began to fight at a dazzling speed.

"Help me to stop them, Benvolio!" pleaded Romeo. He caught Mercutio from behind, pinning his arms to his sides. As he did so, Tybalt lunged forward and drove the point of his rapier through Mercutio's heart, fatally wounding him.

"A plague on both your houses," he whispered with his dying breath.

When Romeo realised that his friend was dead, rage surged through him and his hatred of the Capulets brought a bitter taste to his mouth. "Tybalt!" he cried, drawing his rapier. "One of us must join Mercutio in death!"

"Then let our swords decide who it shall be!" Tybalt snarled.

Romeo hacked at Tybalt as though Tybalt were a tree that he wanted to cut down. At first, the watching Capulets laughed at Romeo's clumsiness, but as Tybalt began to fall back towards the centre of the square, their laughter died. It was obvious that Tybalt was tiring and finding it difficult to defend himself.

At last, Romeo and Tybalt stood face to face, their swords locked together. Tybalt's left hand fumbled at his belt and he drew out a dagger. Romeo, seeing the danger, clamped his left hand around Tybalt's wrist, and they stumbled and struggled with each other.

Tybalt flicked out a foot, intending to trip Romeo, but instead he lost his own balance and the two enemies tumbled to the ground. Romeo fell on Tybalt's left hand, forcing the point of the dagger deep into Tybalt's chest. He felt Tybalt's dying breath warm against his cheek.

A voice called out, "Quick! The Prince's guards!" and the Capulets scattered.

Benvolio helped Romeo to his feet.
"Come now, before it is too late," he said,
but Romeo did not hear him. He stared at
Tybalt's body, and the full realisation of
what he had done fell on him like a weight.

'I have killed Juliet's cousin!' he thought. 'She cannot love a murderer! She will never forgive me! How could I have let myself be such a fool!'

He was still staring at Tybalt when the Prince's guards reached him.

* * *

That night, the Prince of Verona passed judgement on Romeo. "The hatred of the Montagues and Capulets has cost two lives today," he said. "I want no more bloodshed. I will spare Romeo his life, but I banish him to the city of Mantua. He must leave tonight, and if he is ever found in Verona again, he will be put to death!"

* * *

40

When Friar Lawrence heard the news of Romeo's banishment, he was deeply upset. He had already married Romeo and Juliet in secret, hoping that one day, their love would overcome the hatred between the Montagues and the Capulets – but it seemed that the hate had been too strong. After his evening meal, the Friar went to his chapel to say a prayer for the young lovers.

As he knelt in front of the altar, Friar Lawrence heard the sound of the chapel door opening, and footsteps racing up the aisle. He stood, turned and saw Juliet, who flung herself sobbing at his feet.

"Help me, Friar Lawrence!" she begged. "My father wants me to marry Count Paris, but I'd rather die than forsake Romeo."

"Do not despair, my child," Friar Lawrence urged. "Surely you can reason with your father?"

"I could not bring myself to tell him about Romeo," Juliet sobbed. "I pleaded Tybalt's death had made me too full of grief to think of marriage. But Father would not listen and the wedding is to take place tomorrow."

Friar Lawrence looked troubled. "There may be a way for you and Romeo to be together, my child, but it is dangerous," he said.

Friar Lawrence took a tiny bottle of blue liquid from the pouch at his belt. "Drink this tonight," he said, "and you will fall into a sleep as deep as death. Your parents will believe that you are dead and will put your body into the Capulet tomb – but in two days you will wake, alive and well."

"And Romeo?" said Juliet.

"I will send him a message explaining everything," said Friar Lawrence. "After you wake, you can go to Mantua in secret."

* * *

And so, on the morning of Juliet's wedding to Paris, the screams of her nurse woke the whole Capulet house.

When the news of Juliet's death reached Benvolio, he rode straight to Mantua to Romeo. One of the travellers he passed on the way was a monk, who recognised him. "Lord Benvolio!" he called out as Benvolio approached.

"I have a letter for your cousin Romeo from Friar Lawrence!"

"Out of my way!" Benvolio shouted back. "I have no time to stop!"

The monk watched as Benvolio galloped by on the road to Mantua. At that speed, the monk judged, Benvolio would be in the city before evening.

* * *

When Benvolio told Romeo that Juliet was dead, Romeo's heart broke and for hours he lay sobbing on his bed, while outside day turned into night. During that time, Benvolio stayed at Romeo's side, but he had no idea how to comfort his grief-stricken friend.

It was almost midnight before Romeo grew calm enough to speak. He sat up and wiped away his tears with the back of his hand. "I must go to her," he said.

"But the Prince has banished you!" Benvolio reminded him. "If you are seen on the streets of Verona, it will mean your death."

"I am not afraid of death," said Romeo. "Without Juliet, my life means nothing. Go wake the grooms, and tell them to saddle my horse."

When Benvolio
had left him
alone, Romeo
searched through
the wooden chest
at the foot of his
bed until he found
a green glass bottle that
contained a clear liquid. "I shall drink this
poison, and die at Juliet's side!" he vowed.

Romeo left Mantua at daybreak,
refusing to let Benvolio accompany him.

 Once out of the city, he
travelled along
winding country
tracks so that he
could approach
Verona without
being seen.

It was night when he arrived and with the hood of his cloak drawn up to hide his face, he slipped in unrecognised through the city walls at the main gate.

He went straight to the Capulet tomb, and it was almost as if someone had expected him, for the door was unlocked, and the interior was lit by a burning torch.

Romeo looked around, saw Tybalt's
body, pale as candle wax – then Juliet,
laid out on a marble slab, her death-shroud
as white as a bridal gown. With a cry,
Romeo rushed to her side and covered her

face with kisses and tears. "I cannot live without you," he whispered. "I want your beauty to be the last thing my eyes see. We could not be together in life, my sweet love, but in death, nothing shall part us!"

Romeo drew the cork from the poison bottle and raised it to his lips. He felt the vile liquid sting his throat. Then darkness swallowed him.

For a time, there was no sound except the spluttering of the torch; then Juliet began to breathe. She moaned, opened her eyes, and saw Romeo dead at her side with the empty poison bottle in his hand.

At first, she thought she was dreaming, but when she reached out to touch Romeo's face, and smelled the bitter scent of the poison, she knew that the nightmare was real, and that Friar Lawrence's plan had gone terribly wrong. She cradled Romeo in her arms and rocked him, weeping into his hair.

"If you had only waited a little longer!" Juliet whispered, and she kissed Romeo again and again, desperately hoping that there was enough  poison on his lips that she too might die.

Then she saw the torchlight gleam on the dagger at Romeo's belt. She drew the weapon and pressed its point to her heart. "Now, dagger, take me to my love!" she said, and pushed with all her strength.

Friar Lawrence found the lovers a few hours later. They were huddled together like sleeping children.

When Romeo and Juliet died, the hatred between the Montagues and Capulets died with them. United by grief, the two families agreed that Romeo and Juliet should be buried together. They paid for a statue of the lovers to be set over the grave, and on the base of the statue these words were carved:

There never was a story of more woe
Than this of Juliet and Romeo.

The sun for sorrow will not show his head.
Go hence, to have more talk of these sad things.

The Prince of Verona; V.iii.

Love and Hate in Romeo and Juliet

In *Romeo and Juliet*, Shakespeare weaves together two of the most powerful human emotions, love and hate.

The bitter hatred in *Romeo and Juliet* results from the feud between the Montagues and Capulets, two rich families in the Italian city of Verona. The feud has led to so many gang-fights in the streets that the Prince of Verona has ordered the fighting to stop, on pain of death.

The passionate love comes from Romeo and Juliet, who fall in love at first sight at a ball in the Capulet's house. Juliet is a Capulet, Romeo is a Montague, and the moment their lips meet, their fate is sealed. Tybalt, Juliet's cousin, sees them together and swears to take revenge for what he considers an insult to his family.

Shakespeare shows us how strangely alike love and hate are in the way they make people act without thinking. Hate causes the death of both Mercutio, Romeo's best friend, and Tybalt, Juliet's cousin. Love leads Romeo and Juliet into a chain of tragic events. Their happy wedding sets them on the road to a sorry end.

At the end of the play, the young lovers are dead, and the Montagues and Capulets are brought together at last, united by another powerful emotion – grief. The love and the hate have cancelled each other out, and all that is left is sadness.

Shakespeare and the Globe Theatre

Some of Shakespeare's most famous plays were first performed at the Globe Theatre, which was built on the South Bank of the River Thames in 1599.

Going to the Globe was a different experience from going to the theatre today. The building was roughly circular in shape, but with flat sides: a little like a doughnut crossed with a fifty-pence piece. Because the Globe was an open-air theatre, plays were only put on during daylight hours in spring and summer. People paid a penny to stand in the central space and watch a play, and this part of the audience became known as 'the groundlings' because they stood on the ground. A place in the tiers of seating beneath the thatched roof, where there was a slightly better view and less chance of being rained on, cost extra.

The Elizabethans did not bath very often and the audiences at the Globe were smelly. Fine ladies and gentlemen in the more expensive seats sniffed perfume and bags of sweetly-scented herbs to cover the stink rising from the groundlings.

There were no actresses on the stage; all the female characters in Shakespeare's plays would have been acted by boys, wearing wigs and make-up. Audiences were not well-behaved. People clapped and cheered when their favourite actors came on stage; bad actors were jeered at and sometimes pelted with whatever came to hand.

Most Londoners worked hard to make a living and in their precious free time they liked to be entertained. Shakespeare understood the magic of the theatre so well that today, almost four hundred years after his death, his plays still cast a spell over the thousands of people that go to see them.

Orchard Classics

Shakespeare Stories

RETOLD BY ANDREW MATTHEWS
ILLUSTRATED BY TONY ROSS

Orchard Classics are available from all good bookshops,
or can be ordered direct from the publisher:
Orchard Books, PO BOX 29, Douglas IM99 1BQ
Credit card orders please telephone 01624 836000
or fax 01624 837033
or e-mail: bookshop@enterprise.net for details.

To order please quote title, author and ISBN
and your full name and address.
Cheques and postal orders should be
made payable to 'Bookpost plc'.
Postage and packing is FREE within the UK
(overseas customers should add £1.00 per book).

Prices and availability are subject to change.